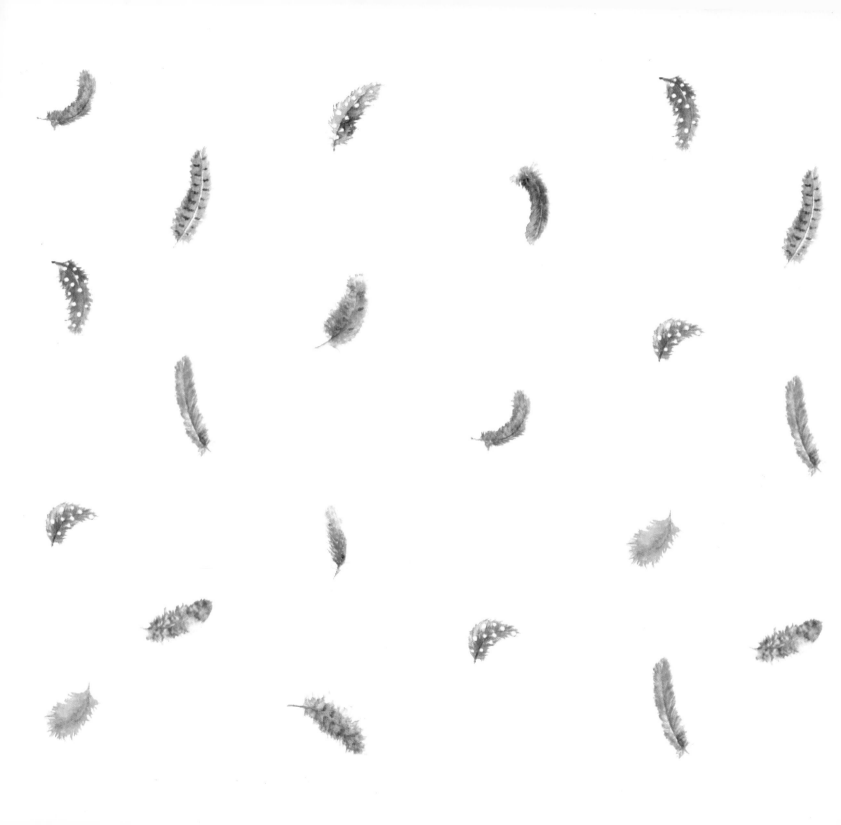

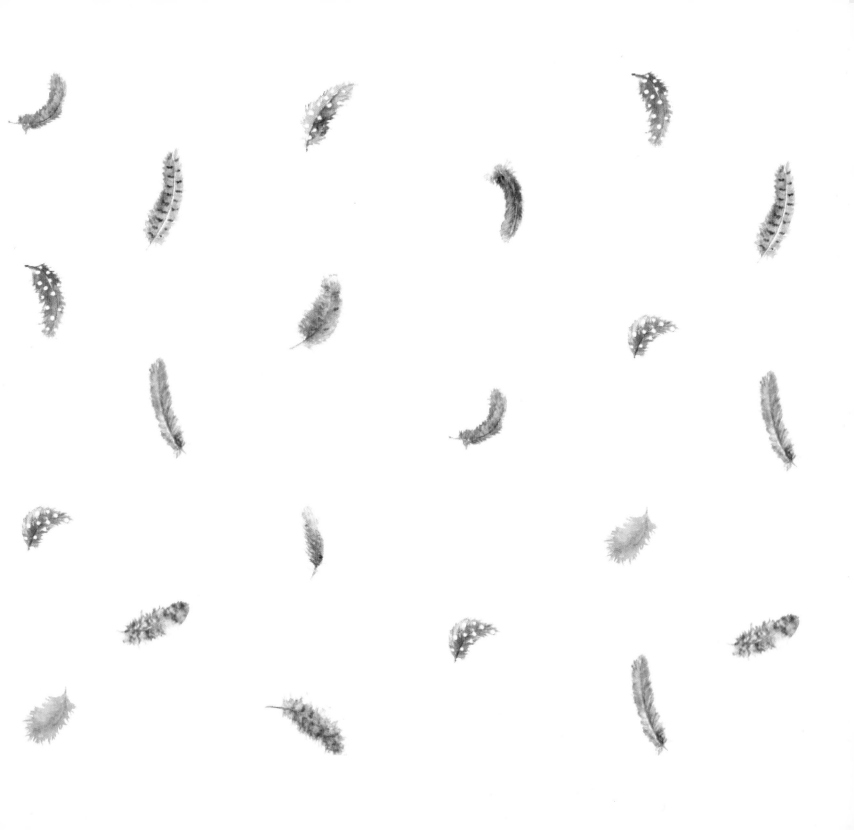

For my parents

my children

my husband

and two hamsters!

First edition for the United States and the Philippines
published by Barron's Educational Series, Inc., 1998

Text and illustrations copyright © Deborah Inkpen, 1998

First published 1998 by Hodder Children's Books

The right of Deborah Inkpen to be recognized as Author of this work has been asserted
by her in accordance with the Copyright, Designs and Patents Act 1988.

All inquiries should be addressed to:
Barron's Educational Series, Inc.
250 Wireless Boulevard
Hauppauge, New York 11788

International Standard Book No. 0-7641-0575-2

Library of Congress Catalog Card No. 97-74869

PRINTED IN HONG KONG/CHINA

9 8 7 6 5 4 3

HARRIET

DEBORAH INKPEN

BARRON'S

Harriet had escaped. Her cage was old. Some of the bars were bent.

She had gnawed at them with her teeth, pushed at them with her paws, and eventually they had moved, just enough.

And now she was free.

Before her lay a huge carpet of green. Above her, giant plants spread their leafy fingers. And over them all stretched the blue sky.

Harriet's whiskers quivered. Her nose twitched. The air was full of new sounds and new smells.

She scampered along the garden path, nosing this way and that.

A dark shadow passed above her. Harriet scurried for cover. The shadow flew into a tree and started to sing.

A rich earthy scent led Harriet into the vegetable patch. She nibbled a spiky leaf. It tasted strange.

Then she nibbled some lettuce. That tasted good.

The carrots and the cabbages were good, too.

But she didn't like the slugs. They were horrible.

Harriet paused to sniff the air. A weedy, watery smell made her feel thirsty.

She followed the smell to the edge of a murky pond.

As she leaned over to drink, a big warty toad popped up its head.

Harriet jumped!
And went plummeting into the pond.

Plop!

The little hamster bobbed to the surface like a cork. The water was cold and full of green, slimy weed that clung to her fur.

Gasping and spluttering, she paddled to the edge and scrambled out,

a tiny,

soggy,

angry heap of fur.

The tiny heap of fur shook itself, smoothed down its coat, cleaned its whiskers, and turned back into a little hamster.

Harriet yawned sleepily.

"Here's a good place to sleep," thought Harriet. Under the apple tree were lots of small holes. Something disappeared into one of them.

She peered down the hole.
A small face looked out.
It stared at Harriet with
black, beady eyes.

"You can't come in here," said a little gray mouse. "Only mice live here."

"You're not a mouse," said another. "You haven't got a tail."

"What are you?" asked a third.

Harriet told them that she was a hamster and that she did have a tail. She turned around to show them. They seemed unimpressed.

"There's no room for hamsters here," they said. "Only mice." And they vanished down their hole.

H arriet tried sleeping inside a flowerpot,
but the cobwebs stuck to her whiskers.

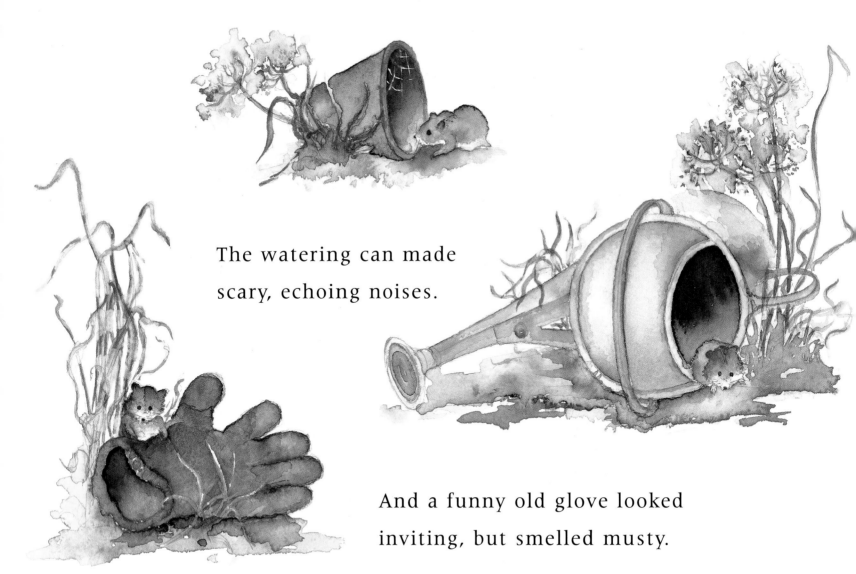

The watering can made
scary, echoing noises.

And a funny old glove looked
inviting, but smelled musty.

Near the apple tree was a compost heap.
Harriet nosed her way inside. It was dark
and warm.

"Perhaps this will be a good place to sleep,"
she thought.

But she had not seen the large,
prickly shape buried under
the leaves.

The hedgehog did not
like being awakened.
It uncurled itself,
grunting angrily,
and rushed
at Harriet.

arriet ran across the open lawn, tripping and rolling and running again. Some wire netting blocked her path. She pushed her nose underneath and wriggled through.

Scrambling up the side of a low wooden shed, she found herself on the roof. She scampered this way and that, looking for a place to hide.

Under the eaves was a dark hole. Harriet scrambled through and tumbled into darkness.

"Squawk!" A huge, foolish-faced creature flapped its wings and rushed around the coop.

Harriet dived beneath a nest of warm eggs and watched as hens scattered in every direction.

Gradually the noise died down. The air began to clear. A big, fat, feathery body plumped down on top of her.

She snuggled back, feeling safe and warm. And at last she fell asleep.

Harriet did not awaken when the hen left the nest. She did not awaken when chubby fingers began to collect the eggs. Nor did she awaken when a delighted voice squealed,

"There you are, Harriet!"

The sleepy little hamster was placed carefully into an egg basket.

"Come on then," said the voice. "Let's take you home."

But Harriet did not hear.
She did not even stir.

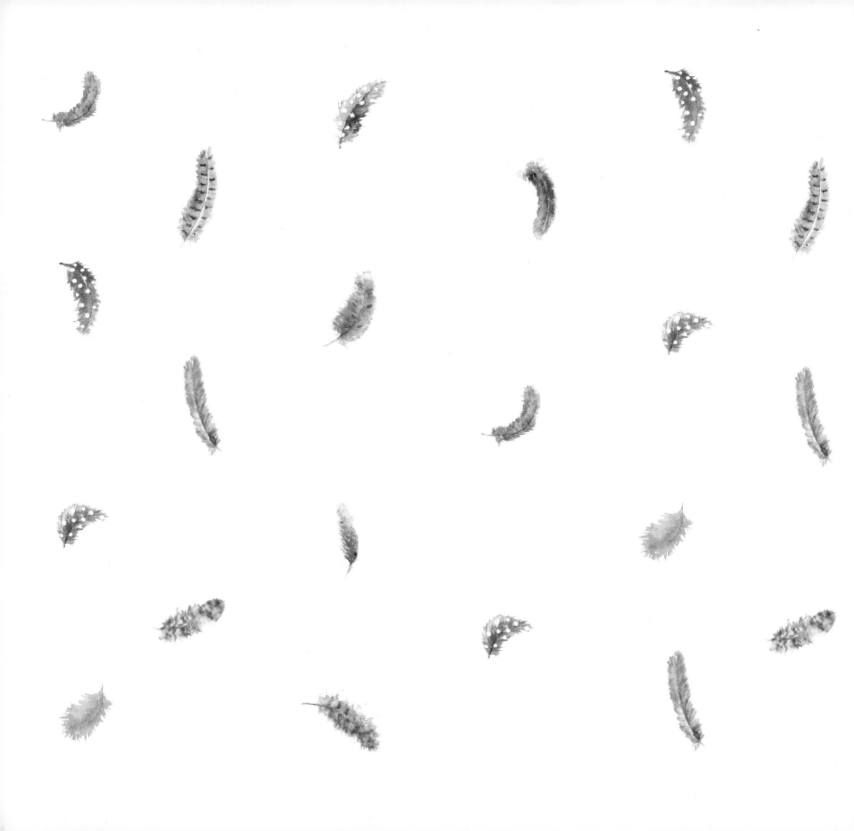

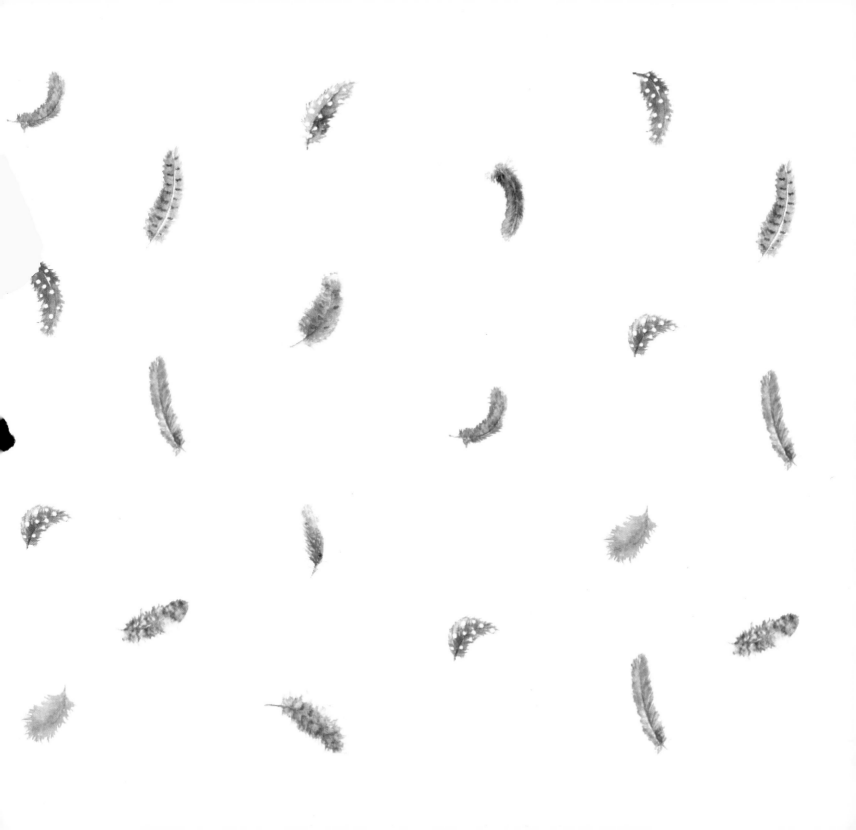